R

Home

Anatiposi

Ray Palmer

Home

Reprint of the original, first published in 1872.

1st Edition 2023 | ISBN: 978-3-38212-958-3

Anatiposi Verlag is an imprint of Outlook Verlagsgesellschaft mbH.

Verlag (Publisher): Outlook Verlag GmbH, Zeilweg 44, 60439 Frankfurt, Deutschland
Vertretungsberechtigt (Authorized to represent): E. Roepke, Zeilweg 44, 60439 Frankfurt, Deutschland
Druck (Print): Books on Demand GmbH, In de Tarpen 42, 22848 Norderstedt, Deutschland

HOME;

OR,

THE UNLOST PARADISE.

BY

RAY PALMER.

NEW YORK:
ANSON D. F. RANDOLPH AND COMPANY,
770 BROADWAY.
1872.

Press of
JOHN WILSON AND SON,
Cambridge.

Bindery of
ROBERT RUTTER,
82 *and* 84 *Beekman St.*,
NEW YORK.

TO THE

Mothers and Daughters of Our Country,

ON WHOM CHIEFLY THE REALIZATION OF THE DIVINE IDEA OF THE FAMILY AND HOME MUST DEPEND;

WHOSE HIGHEST DISTINCTION IT IS TO MAKE HUMANITY COMPLETE; TO ELEVATE, PURIFY AND ADORN DOMESTIC LIFE; AND TO BLESS ALIKE CHILDHOOD, MATURITY AND AGE, WITH SWEET AND TENDER MINISTRIES;

THESE PAGES ARE MOST RESPECTFULLY INSCRIBED BY

THE AUTHOR.

PREFACE.

THIS POEM was conceived and partly executed several years ago; but through the constant pressure of official labors, it has lain uncompleted till a recent date. Perhaps the delay has been no real disadvantage, since special circumstances have of late given fresh interest, and, if possible, enhanced importance to the theme.

The writer has desired to present such a picture of Home as not only may be, but actually has been, substantially realized in instances almost without number. The sketch is supposed to have had its original in New England, — not because such Homes are not now widely found beyond her boundaries, but because, historically, our American Homes there first exhibited their highest moral power and beauty; so that it may be fairly claimed that from her, as its source, has flowed the purest and best social life of our country. The early settlers laid the foundations of society in learning and religion; and it may reasonably be doubted whether there has ever been another spot of equal extent on the globe, in which so great a number of intelligent and virtuous Homes could have been counted. The healthful influence of New England domestic life now reaches the newly rising States to the very shores of the Pacific.

To those who have known the joys and permanent benefits of well-ordered and happy Homes, the writer trusts that the reading of these pages may afford a tranquil pleasure. It is well to revive and cherish the sweet recollections of childhood and youth, to recall the vicissitudes of after years, and to bring back the dear faces of the loved and honored who have passed away from earth. Such reminiscences tend to make the heart better.

If what has here been written shall help, even in the least degree, to elevate in the minds of young men and women the ideal of the family and Home, and to deepen in the hearts of any a conviction of the sacredness and beauty of a pure domestic life and the peril to every interest of humanity involved in the desecration of household sanctities, the author will thankfully recognize the accomplishment of his highest purpose.

CONTENTS.

PART I.

PART II.

PART III.

PART IV.

PART I.

Domestic happiness, thou only bliss
Of Paradise that has survived the fall!

Cowper.

Love is life's end: an end but never ending;
All joys, all sweets, all happiness awarding;
Love is life's wealth, ne'er spent but ever spending,
More rich by giving, taking by discarding;
Love's life's reward, rewarded in rewarding.

Spenser.

HOME.

PART I.

COME, gentle lyre! sequestered from the world,
Tired of its tumults and its pomps and pride,
Thee, wonted solace of my careworn heart,
Glad I resume: intent not now to strike
With hurried hand thy strings, nor thee to make
Loud resonant of numbers strange or wild;
But, with such mood serene and airy touch
As best befit soft-breathing harmonies,
To wake thy tones on a familiar theme.

As whom necessity ordains to tread
The arid waste where trackless Libyan sands
Reflect the sun, seek not in vain to find,
At distant intervals, some friendly spots

Where gurgling waters 'neath o'ershadowing palms
Invite repose; so, o'er the wastes of life
While sent to roam, where pines full oft unfilled
Intense desire, and nameless ills beset
Us hapless wanderers on an unknown way,
We seek and find oases bright and fair.

Most fair, most bright, art thou, dear peaceful Home.
Of all best earthly gifts by Heaven bestowed
Man's pilgrim path to cheer. Ever thou art
A refuge from the storm; from the rough wind
A covert. All who may, in each dark hour
When sorrows bow the soul, or when of care
The lighter burden wearily doth press,
Fly to thy bosom, and secluded find
In thy sweet influence solace and repose.
Who know thee not — alas, that such should be! —
Pine for thee, and still hope, though hope deferred
Hath oft made sick the heart, that yet for them
Some spot shall bear thy well-beloved name.
The wanderer thinks of thee. With him he bears

A thousand hallowed memories, fondly kept,
That waken oft afresh. E'en while he treads,
With heedful musings, old historic ground,
Rich with the spoils of Time, where crumbling stand
The hoary monuments of glories dead;
Or climbs 'mid Alpine wonders, and surveys
Rude wilds where Nature all untamed abides;
In search of thee his truant thought will stray.
Or if he tempt the main, far, far away
Swept by the breeze across the heaving deep,
Fixed on his lonely watch at midnight hour,
The watery waste around, the stars above,
Back o'er the flood he roams to visit thee.
For thee the captive sighs in the still gloom
Of his dim cell. The warrior grim, what time
He treads the battle-field where marshalled hosts
Await the bloody fray — pride on his brow
And glory on his crest — lets fall a tear,
While o'er him steal, like flute-notes faintly heard,
Remembrances thick-coming of thy joys.
Dear rest and centre thou of faithful hearts,

Where'er thy seat; as well 'neath tropic suns
As where Arcadian realms boast genial skies,
Or arctic winter spreads eternal snows;
O'er the wide world thy magic spell enchains.

Not many years have rolled since, where now smile
New England's happy Homes, the forest stood,
A mighty wilderness. O'er hills and vales
Spread virgin groves, where never yet had rung
The stroke of woodman's axe, and tangled brakes
And thickets dark, that many a covert wove.
There prowled the cruel wolf. There undisturbed
The bear reared her fierce progeny. The owl
Hooted from his lone seat upon the pine,
And echo answered back. The eagle soared
And screamed, or, pouncing on his quivering prey,
Perched on some naked cliff and fed secure.
Along the river, gliding broad and slow,
Or up the rapid brook, that babbling loud
Rushed from the mountain headlong to the plain,
The trout and salmon darted unensnared.

Of human kind sole tenant of the wild,
The lordly savage reigned, and urged the chase,
Of useful toil impatient; or, when war
Roused his dark passions, from his ambuscade
Treacherous he darted, and, with horrid yell,
Vengeful and unrelenting scalped his foe.
No peaceful Home was then. The dingy squaw,
The menial of her lord, now left to guard
The smoky wigwam, now with blows compelled
Him vagrant to attend with weary load,
Dragged out, a semi-brute, her wretched life.

For man, for woman, God all-good ordained
A worthier destiny. By sacred ties,
In household life and harmony of love
He formed them to be joined; society
Made sure by nature's law; and so decreed
That states and kingdoms should successive rise;
That mind with mind in sympathy should wake
New energies, the needs of men impel
To foster arts, and search creation through

For knowledge of his own eternal thoughts.
He meant not the prolific earth should lie
Incultivate, but, tilled with patient care,
Should smile with flowers as erst an Eden smiled,
And yield the culturing hand a rich reward.
'Twas His behest that bade the forest bow,
The savage beast retire, and savage men
Give place to cultivation, order, laws.

A lonely bark came o'er the stormy sea;
Not freighted deep with pelf: it richer bore,
What famed Golconda's treasures could not buy,
A band of noble hearts. Men trod that deck
Who knew that they were men, and freely gave
For liberty and truth what else was dear.
No factious spirits, who, through spleen or pride,
Contemned their country's laws and roamed to find
What earth's circumference within, for them,
Was nowhere to be found, content and peace.
Of England's best, to her they fondly clung,
Proud of her glorious names and old renown;

And as her loyal sons their lives had spent,
And with her honored dead had peaceful slept
'Neath hallowed aisles in storied chapels dim,
Less had they loved what most ennobles man —
Freedom of soul, pure faith, and peace with heaven.
Hatred hath called them stern; their sturdy strength
Of principle hath bigotry misnamed;
And levity, with leer and jibe profane,
Blasphemed their sanctity and saintly zeal.
'Tis rather bigotry that dares deny
Their nobleness, their glory that would stain.
Warm were their hearts; none warmer e'er did beat
In manly breasts; and humble though their Homes,
By hard necessity, yet love and beauty there
Found place for sweet unfolding, nor was mirth
A stranger at those hearths where nightly blazed
The fires that made a fireside worth the name.
Knowledge, religion, virtue — wheresoe'er
These dwell together, dwell earth's best delights.
Not faultless were they, else were they not men;
Yet less their own the faults than of their time;

Of times long past, when many an error reigned
As yet unchallenged, blinding all alike
To truths since seen as in the midday blaze.
Beyond their fellows, keenly had they pierced
Error's thick-veiling mists, and Truth discerned
In her diviner forms; aside had flung
Falsehoods long honored, maxims cherished long
That mighty ills had wrought; the good, the right,
In their great hearts they worshipped; these they sought,
As misers search for gold, with deathless love;
Clung to them found, as with the grasp of fate!
What if perchance from ardor so intense
Of quenchless earnestness, their zeal o'erglowed
At times, and they — their vision not yet clear —
There erred where all the world had erred till then?
Ah! ye who meanly seek to tear away
The honors thickly clustered round their brows,
Yours — yours the lack of heavenly charity
Ye charge on them; yours with far less defence!
On you returned at last shall rest the shame;

And as the sun from the clear mirror wipes
The envious vapor that its lustre dimmed,
Just Time their names to honor shall restore.*

Such were thy sires, New England; such the men
That tamed thy wilds; thy slopes and valleys robed
With waving fields; made e'en thy rugged hills
Look kind; thy teeming cities with their marts,
Their industries and commerce, rise and thrive.
Rich among lands art thou in sweet content,
In health and plenty, born of patient toil.
Rich in thy stalwart sons and daughters fair,
That o'er the world, where'er their feet may tread,
Bear with them blessing. Known of all are they,
Of keen intelligence and purpose firm.
About their footsteps truth and freedom spring,
And law's firm voice is heard — her word obeyed;
Wide sown are wisdom's seeds, and useful arts,
With many a curious, many a rare device,
Lend force to labor, or embellish life.

---

* See Appendix, note A.

Their Mother they forget not; but from far,
Where, ocean-like, the boundless Prairie spreads,
Where rock-ribbed mountains lift their frowning forms,
And sunset regions kiss the western wave,
Their hearts with many a yearning backward turn,
True to her still; and all her scenes recalled
Look fairer seen in memory's mellow light.
A Holy Land she seems, where God abides;
Nor seems alone. Holy well named a land
Where lives a faith divine; where graceful rise
Religion's hallowed domes, and close at hand
The school-house, fit ally, within whose walls
Kind culture early moulds the plastic mind
To virtue and to truth; where stand embowered
The mantled cottage and the tasteful Home.
Dear tranquil scenes! Home, o'er the world a name
That like a talisman calls to the soul
All images of bliss, hath here a spell
Of mightiest working.* Other lands may boast
More friendly soils; and blander airs may breathe

---

* Appendix, note B.

Upon their spicy beds that odors yield
More fragrant far; and birds of rarer note
Among their groves pour richer melodies;
And lordlier dwellings rise. But where hath earth
A soil more free, a clime that ministers
More vigor to the frame, or fosters more
True energy of soul? Where Nature's face
A nobler aspect — mountain crests that climb
In their blue dimness, reverend forests tall
Crowning the hills with majesty and grace,
And waterfalls that, with sonorous voice
Softened by distance, charm the listening ear?
Where doth the rustic dwelling more bespeak
Substantial comfort, or with happier art
Where Luxury convenience blend with taste?

In yon sweet vale that — mingling field and grove
In fair confusion — fills the roving eye
With images of beauty; on a slope
Gently declining toward the midday sun,
A modest mansion stands; a rural Home;

But one of thousands that New England boasts —
The jewels of her crown — her pride and joy.
Nor rude, nor splendid, it hath yet a charm,
A quiet loveliness. Come, ye who dream
That Peace, an exile, dwells with men no more;
Ye who in vain pursue her through the maze
Where witching pleasure lures, and oft deceived
As oft the eager chase again renew;
Ye who would seek her but in princely halls,
With fretted ceiling arched and draperies hung
In gorgeous richness, where luxurious couch
And orient ottoman invite repose,
With harp, or lute, by snowy fingers touched,
That soothes and lulls in soft voluptuous strain —
Come hither, mark, and muse and grow more wise.

Lo, where the hand of taste hath graced the scene!
The charms of nature by judicious skill
Are heightened here; their absence there supplied
By quaint device. The grassy plat that spreads
In neat simplicity before the door,

Majestic elms, by some ancestral hand
Long years ago transplanted, overhang;
Their arching boughs affording grateful shade
To childhood's laughing groups, that gather there
In merry mood, on the bright summer day,
And with their harmless pastimes fill the hours.
The tasteful garden, with neat fence enclosed,
Bespeaks attentive culture. Clustering trees,
The apple, cherry, pear, the tempting peach
And the delicious plum, are set to please
The order-loving eye; and 'mid the shades
Of their dark foliage half conceal the bower,
Round which the woodbine creeps and roses twine.
Here thickly set the grateful currant grows,
And the sweet raspberry. The vine there climbs
O'er the arched trellis; and, when Autumn claims
Her offering of fruits, hangs richly out
Her purple clusters; while yon beds of flowers,
Of many a name and hue, their incense pay
To genial Summer, when they drink her smiles.
Here oft at twilight of a summer's eve,
While linger yet, along the glowing west,

Clouds, that like golden islands seem to float
Upon an azure sea, or spread afar
Like some imperial pavement wrought with art
Divine, of precious stones, agate and amethyst,
Sapphire and emerald — come, arm in arm,
The beautiful and young. The peaceful hour
Sheds its sweet influence o'er them. Slowly now,
As best befits such converse as they hold,
They thread the winding paths, or seek the bower;
And now, as with some sudden transport seized,
Burst forth in merry laugh, and glide along,
Like tripping fairies, in pursuit and flight
Alternate, as capricious impulse moves.
But gay, or grave, alike they waken here,
'Mid outward loveliness, pure thoughts, and feel
Quick-kindling sympathies their hearts unite.
Here, as in earth's first garden, dwells sweet Peace,
With joys of innocence and social love;
A Home is here, with all its histories,
Its storied past, its present, and to come.
O'er it have passed the changing lights and shades,

Or will as years shall run their circles round,
Which, since was lost the primal Paradise,
Have checkered all the mortal lot of men.

Home, 'tis to heaven's wise law we mortals owe
Thee and all thine. In the first Home was placed
Not Adam sole; with him the gentler Eve,
Woman, man's other self, in whom alone
His complement he finds. God called, 'tis said,
Not his, but their name, Adam, in the day
When He humanity complete had made.
E'er since, in thee, O wedded love, are laid
The deep foundations of domestic bliss;
With thee, through all the cycles, have been hid
Sweet springs of joy whence, like full streams, have flowed
Earth's pleasures that are likest those of heaven.
For what is heaven save innocence and love
Inseparable — in mystic life combined? —
The sympathy of hearts that throb and glow
With love's quick impulse, and harmonious beat,

Each vibrating to each, as in the harp
To one touched string according strings respond?
Eternal Love, intent to make earth blest
With all best joys, nor man nor woman made
For unrelated life, but each for each;
Each only in the other without lack
Of somewhat that, unfound, the restless heart
Yearns ever, nor can know a full content.
O subtile instinct! Hidden law deep wrought
Into the soul's own texture, by His will
Who, Love Himself, man in his likeness framed
To dwell in love; his native element,
The vital air, in which to live and move!
God and thy kind both loved with one pure flame,
O mortal, thou most like to God shalt be,
Blessing and blessed; and by thy stony paths
Shall spring such flowers as Paradise did yield
Ere with the reign of love her all she lost.

Yon mansion long ago, one summer morn,
A morn bright, dewy, fresh with balmy breath

Of myriad blossoms laughing o'er the fields,
Received a youthful pair. Late at God's shrine
In holy rite made one, hand joined to hand
As heart before to heart, here they begin,
Rich in fair hopes and visions, and yet more
In fresh affections, for themselves and theirs
A Home to found and consecrate. Henceforth,
Holy the place shall be through opening years,
In all their thoughts; sacred to wedded love,
To tranquil joys, to purity, to peace;
To healthful pleasures with each other shared;
To useful tasks together daily wrought;
To books and culture, and congenial friends;
To piety, and prayer, and heavenward steps;
To all that earth yet yields to faithful hearts
Demonstrative that once an Eden was,
And proof, by foretaste, that a heaven shall be.
Edward and Mary — these the names they bore;
Names, like their story, neither new nor strange.
Nor name nor story such as one might choose
Who with romantic tale, or legend old,

Or startling horror, would the listless rouse;
But suiting well the simple and the true.

O happy man! To whom of God 'tis given
To lead, a joyous bride, one who has taught
Thy heart — that as in fevered restlessness,
Far roving, stayed not till her gentle eye
Seized it and fast a willing captive held —
To end its rovings and in her to rest!
How like an angel in the robes of heaven
She stands beside thee — thine own angel now!
How beats with manly pride thy heart, the while
Thou lead'st her from the altar to the seat,
Her fitting throne, at Home's dear centre placed;
Where, as a queen, ruling without command,
She, radiant as the morning star, shall shine,
Mighty in gentleness, in sweetness strong.
It is but meet that on her maiden brow,
And in the eyes that kindle at thy glance,
Thou shouldst enraptured gaze; and gazing find
Thy soul with nobler manliness inspired,

And high ambitions all unfelt before.
Henceforth, for thee shall each returning dawn
Wake worthiest thoughts. Not for thyself alone,
Thou shalt go forth life's battle-fields to try;
But with chivalric tread and lance in rest,
For her, to death if need, in gallant strife
Thou shalt defend all honor, truth and right;
Win all that may on her true lustre shed;
And shield her from all ills that courage firm,
And strength of love, and patience can avert.
For God and her! What impulse canst thou lack
To wrestle with all dangers, to withstand
Pleasure's seductive call, and Duty's voice
With quenchless ardor ever to obey!

Thou too, O woman, of thy kind most blest,
Who in thy spring of beauty standest glad
Beside thy well beloved and call'st him now
Thy husband! Name so rich to thy fond heart,
In promise of best joys that earth can know.
To thee no music like the bridegroom's voice;

To that thy tremulous heart instant responds,
As to the soft west wind the swelling strain
Waked on the harp-string breathes its sweetness back.
In him thy strength thou seest. The sturdy arm
To which thou cling'st confiding, thine shall be
In danger's hour for succor and defence;
For kind support when on the toilsome way
Thy steps would falter, or thy heart grow faint.
His wisdom, courage, manhood, to thy soul
More nicely strung, with quicker, keener sense
By God endowed, shall healthful reverence wake
And restful confidence; shall teach thy thought
In generous rivalry to tempt the heights
Of intellectual grandeur and to grasp
What best and highest mortal powers may reach,
Of knowledge that exalts and gifts that charm.
Will he repress thee? Ay, as summer suns
Repress the morning rosebud, opening wide
Its bosom to the day and calling forth
Its sweetest odors and its loveliest hues!
Edward and Mary, each in each complete!

Husband and wife, but one Humanity —
One conscious life full-flowing — with one heart,
One will, one end supreme, one blessedness!
'Twas so that God ordained domestic bliss.

Now, with exultant step, from room to room
They wander, and well pleased each trait survey
Of this their new abode — their HOME, when time
And love and joys the place hath sanctified,
When sorrow's shade, perchance, has overhung
And hallowed it, baptized with holy tears,
Till tenderest memories, gathered one by one,
Thick clustering, link each object to the heart.
Like children, whom new toys or pleasures fill
With gushing raptures, they with quick survey
Scan each apartment; try each chair and lounge;
Look from each window on the prospect fair;
Each picture on the garnished walls observe
With keenest glance, as if with critic's eye
In Angelo, or Raphael, they sought
Some touch of grace unnoted e'er before.

But in each other, chiefly, pleased they see
The graces most transcendent; and the light
Of love within suffuses each dear face,
And glows, as when through some fair vase or globe
Translucent softly shines the embosomed flame.

So passed with silent feet the jocund Hours.
Then while this first day of their wedded life
Closed over them serene, and twilight fell,
Hand clasped in hand they sat, till daylight died
And set love's favorite star; too full their hearts
For words; their silent bliss like some sweet dream.
Thus for a time. But when the deepened shade
Their faces veiled, it was as if each tongue
Gained freedom and each heart, unlocked,
Revealed its hidden treasures; and they talked
As ne'er before of all the vanished past,
Of present pleasures and of dawning hopes;
Of all that each to each aspired to be
In the great life-work. Then at last they kneeled
With hearts in true accord before the throne,

Their Father's throne of pure eternal love,
And in His name who bore the bitter cross
Forgiveness sought and breathed their praise to heaven.
Angels! to whom of God the task is given
With loving ministries, though all unseen, to watch
And keep, with care unwearied, every hour,
The heirs of life whose souls in love abide;
Ye at that hour were nigh. Ye saw them bow
And worship; heard those fervent lips declare
That God should be their God; heard them entreat
That He whom heaven itself, the heaven of heavens,
Could not contain, would with them deign to dwell,
Gladdening their Home and hearts with that same smile
That gladdens all above; would own them His,
Them and their household, and in trouble's day,
Or when thick perils should beset them round,
Such as must come to all, comfort and rest
Beneath the shadow of his wings would give.
Ye saw — for ye have spiritual vision clear —
How rose their warm affections to the throne,

As when of old the smoke of incense, cast
On glowing altars, rose in circling wreaths,
And He who dwelt between the cherubim
Smelled a sweet savor. Thou thyself didst hear,
Thou without whom not e'en the sparrow falls;
The trust Thou didst accept, and didst command
Thy blessing; charge to all good angels Thou
Didst give, by night and day, with ceaseless guard
All evils to forefend, save such as needs
Must be for Virtue's sake, that ever best
Thrives while she wrestles, by thy grace made strong.
Henceforth, thrice happy pair, although for you
Each day new cares may spring and duty set
New tasks, with these shall come celestial Peace,
And, where God dwells and dear domestic love,
Shall nestle and abide. Earth's purest joys,
Unsating because pure, there fresh shall spring
As o'er you swiftly pass the fleeting years;
Till from this earthly Home ye pass to heaven.

PART II.

I SAW her upon nearer view,
A Spirit, yet a Woman too!
Her household motions light and free,
And steps of virgin liberty;
A countenance in which did meet
Sweet records, promises as sweet;
A creature not too bright or good
For human nature's daily food;
For transient sorrows, simple wiles,
Praise, blame, love, kisses, tears, and smiles.

Wordsworth.

THERE are smiles and tears in the mother's eyes,
For her new born babe beside her lies;
O heaven of bliss! when the heart o'erflows
With the rapture a *mother only* knows!

Henry Ware, Jr.

PART II.

O JOY of joys! the joy of wedded hearts,
That at God's shrine in youthful freshness joined,
Are one for ever — mystery of love!
Thenceforth, like two clear fountains side by side,
That pour their waters into one bright stream,
They blend their free affections, till the tide,
In one deep channel, floweth ever on.
As in green meadows by some river's side,
Spring 'neath the sun daisy and violet,
With many a peer, of many a name and tinge,
And blossom numberless to grace the scene;
So where that sacred current affluent glides
Through the charmed valley of domestic bliss,
Shoot forth all virtues that humanity
Do most adorn and beauty lend to life.
Here sheltered, they may bud and bloom secure

From beasts that raven the wide world abroad;
In rich luxuriance grow, and crown thee, Home,
With graces that most charm the pure in heart.
No cynic eye thy secrecy invades,
To note, and noting check, love's language true,
That half unconsciously, with artless art,
And simplest act, some secret meaning tells.
A gentle word; a glance; perchance a kiss;
Or whate'er slightest ministry may prove
Expressive of the fulness that o'erflows
Each happy heart — so hours as minutes fly!
In this, his fortress, Love in freedom reigns;
Commands, obeys, nor to distinguish knows
Duty and pleasure, since they here are one.

Now wakes the morn — Nature's great miracle,
Repeated ever, yet for ever new —
When start afresh the busy wheels of life,
That through night's silent reign awhile stood still.
Listen! what mingled sounds swell on the ear,
While kindle Nature's slumbers into smiles!

The groves, but now so still, grow vocal, and pour forth
From thousand tuneful throats such melodies
As might e'en Dulness, drowsy maid, herself
Awake to ecstasy. June's unmown fields
Stand tremulous, all wet with silvery dew,
Night's grateful benison. The clouds that hung
Like parting curtains when the day awoke,
Transfigured, glow as dipped in Tyrian dyes
Of hue celestial — ruby, jasper, gold.
The chariot of the King of Day they seem,
In which, with pomp ascending o'er the heights,
He climbs the noonward path. The wreathing mists
That hide, and yet reveal, the stream that winds
Along the quiet valley, slowly lift,
Like beauty's veil, and show the grace beneath.
The voice of flocks and herds that hasten forth
Eager to taste the pasture blend confused,
Yet please the listening ear. The flowery train,
With which bright Summer loves at early dawn
Her retinue to fill, spread o'er the fields,

Entincturing with their breath the roving wind
That wooes them in their sweetness, while they seem,
As if in conscious life, to glow with joy.
These, Morning, are thy charms; and ever new,
From bounding childhood down to tottering age,
To hearts with inborn tenderness endowed,
And natures finely tuned, they yield delight.

Yet 'tis when hearts most leap with gladsome life,
And passion's impulses; with eager hopes,
Imaginations, fancies, visions, dreams,
And, born of these, emotions, like pent fires
That will not be repressed, but force their way:
'Tis when youth's throbbing pulses send their blood
Swift coursing through the veins, and every sense
And sensibility is quick and keen;
'Tis most of all when love, pure, happy love,
So permeates with its subtile force the breast,
That thought and purpose, sympathy and will,
Delighted own its sway; oh, yes! 'tis then
That most the world enrobes itself in light,

With beauty all suffused; that morn and eve,
Sun, moon, and stars, and ocean, lake, and stream,
Woods, hills, and fields, and all earth's features fair,
Seem as incarnadined with roseate hues,
And through the liquid air there seems to float
A glory, that intoxicates the soul
With dreamy bliss, and to the softened heart
Makes Nature's simplest, lowliest work divine.

'Twas thus exultant and elate, that morn,
That Edward stood, with Mary at his side,
And from the casement gazed, with open heart
Drinking all sweetness from the radiant scene,
Through every sense; while in her beaming face
He saw reflected his own tranquil joy.
To both, on this their wedded life's first day,
With omens kind begun, ne'er looked before
The world so beautiful; ne'er God himself,
The Infinite Creator, seemed so good.
And while, with the ascending sun, went up
From off the dewy earth the morning mists,

Rising like incense, from their tuneful lips
And hearts o'erflowing, rose their hymn of praise
With fervent orisons to listening Heaven,
Whither no voice of love ascends in vain.

Is then the goal attained? Is this retreat —
The dream of many a year at last fulfilled —
A bower of ease, in which, with lotus charm,
The past may be forgot; the future, veiled
In golden haze, be all unquestioned left,
And purpose high in pleasure's cup be drowned?
No! In the blissful shades where primal man
Walked innocent with God, 'twas given to dress
And keep the garden — toil no natural ill.
For use, O mortal, God thy powers hath given,
And made their use a joy. In labors meet,
Pursued for virtue's ends, in good achieved
And triumphs won by sacrifice, by love
Enlarged and with all generous yearnings filled,
Thou shalt such pleasures find as most exalt
Thy being and thy restless soul compose.

Not by ignoble ease, but noble deeds,
Thou dost reveal the spirit all divine
That in thee lives and makes thee like to God
And brother of the angels, who, as winds
And flames of fire, are swift to work his will;
For thee, as them, to serve is to be blest.

Home hath its tasks. Each day demands anew
The thoughtful purpose and the skilful hand.
Thou, Mary, now crowned queen of this fair realm,
Must wield thy sceptre and with gentle grace,
Grace that to thee is power, shouldst wield it well.
'Tis thine this Home to fashion as thou wilt;
To give it thine own impress, till it seems
Pervaded by thy spirit — full of thee!
'Tis thine to guard its order, beauty, health;
To keep it ever free from passion's jar
And discord's grating tones, nor e'er permit
The clamors of the rude and noisy world
Its quiet to invade. Here thou hast power,
By thine own magic arts, o'er all to shed

The living air of joy, that whoso breathes
Shall seem, as by enchantment, warmed and filled
With genial gladness. Here, by thee beguiled,
The troubled brow shall lose its furrows, deep
By cares inwrought; the heavy heart grow light
And gather strength and courage for new toils.
Music with sounding string and richest strain,
And Poesy with all her visions rare,
And kindred arts whose simplest gifts may please,
Shall blend their charms to grace thy queenly state,
Obedient to thy summons. Nor shall Mirth
Withhold her ringing laugh when thou shalt call;
But, with all innocent pleasures in her train,
Shall come to visit thee and lend her aid
To make thy court earth's fairest, happiest spot.

Yet not to listless ease, nor pleasure's round,
The life inane that pampered luxury
Elsewhere delights to lead, thy realm be given.
This is thy pride, New England, that thy Homes
With healthful industries did e'er abound.

Thy matrons, in the halcyon days of yore,
Lived not alone to order well their house
And ply the needle, but with vigorous grasp
Wielded the loom; and from the distaff drew
With busy hand and foot the flaxen thread;
Carded the wool and twirled the humming wheel.
O days of sweet content! No need was then
That commerce rifle every foreign strand
From India to Peru, with raiment meet
Brought from afar, the household to attire.
If of this glory thou no more canst boast
As thou wast wont—so times and manners change—
Yet are thy dwellings Industry's abode;
Her name is honored there. So let it be,
Till Plymouth Rock itself shall waste with years!

Yes, Mary! If a queen thou hast been crowned,
Forget not that with crowns there needs must come
Duty and care. Life opens now to thee
Its long perspective, and arrayed thou seest,
Far stretching on before, its years of toil;

Pleasing, not terrible, the vision seems.
Thou wouldst not live a cipher. Thy young heart
Throbs with its eagerness a part to bear,
Some worthy part, among the good and brave
Who live to conquer ill, and love the strifes
Whose prize is gladness and whose fruits are Peace.
No weak ambition thine to send thy name
Resounding, like an echo, through the world;
Made common on all lips, sullied perchance
By its rude contacts, and its fragrance lost!
Wiser, thou choosest in the tranquil sphere
Of dear domestic peace, by duty done
To grave thine image on the loving hearts
That gather round thee, to thine influence sweet
Opening, as lilies on the placid stream
Bare their fair bosoms to the grateful sun.
Nobler thou deem'st the task, that manly heart
Now knit to thine, beyond all chance to hold
Loyal to thee and restful in thy truth;
To make thyself his ever conscious want,
His life's chief joy; nor, striving, shalt thou fail

O'er him to throw thy spells. Thy morning smile
Will sweetly haunt him through the livelong hours.
E'en 'mid the din of business, on his ear
Will steal thy tones. As thou each day for him,
So he for thee, shall think and plan and toil.
Wealth, honor, fame — whate'er of either crowns
His patient strivings, most of all for thee
His thought will prize; and nightly at thy feet,
With noble pride, he will exulting lay
The trophies he has won. Or if perchance,
In the rough contacts of a restless world,
Where thickly, oft, keen shafts of malice fly,
He hath been wounded sore; if on him fall
Misfortune's lowering shade, with doubt and dread
That tire the soul with watching, and his heart,
Firm though it be, half faints; he then to thee
Shall turn for strength and healing; and thy voice,
Thy cheering glance, thy counsels and thy prayer,
Shall nerve him all anew; with ardor fired
Shall send him to the battle's front again,
New triumphs in heroic strife to win.

Thou too shalt own his power. As he to thee
Shall turn for love's deep tenderness, and warm
Each day anew his heart at the pure flame
That, as on vestal altars, ever glows
Within thy breast; so thou when burdens press,
Or dangers gather thick, in him shall see
Thy helper strong; and ever by his side
More surely thou shalt scale the rugged steeps
And passes perilous that wait thy feet.
In his life thou shalt live, and so become
Worthy of high companionship and meet,
Sharing his struggles, with him to be crowned.
Each year shall thus thy being's measure fill,
The treasures hidden in thy soul unlock,
And make thee rich in dignity and grace,
And all that most exalts; till thou, the wife,
Shalt stand confessed the glory of the man
Thy husband, and he thine; by trial each
Proved to the other equal, helper, friend.

Oh, lightly dance the hours, and swift the day
Speeds round its circuit, if the heart be glad!
When with the frequent task and press of care
Come many a kindly impulse, born of love,
And many a fantasy, that warm the soul
With ever fresh delight; when sympathies
Seem e'en, like odors that exhale, to rise
Spontaneous, and to breathe themselves abroad
As if from sheer exuberance; and there flits
Before affection's eye the image fair
Of a dear face that absence cannot hide; —
Then, Time, thou turn'st in vain thy flowing glass,
To mark thy flight; no note the sand receives!
'Tis so that in that Home days seem but hours,
And weeks but days, and months, as weeks, go by.
The blithesome wife guides all with patient skill,
And taste that seems an instinct; fain to make
Parlor and library, each several room,
Each mantle, niche and arch, or deep recess,
Fair with chaste beauty, grateful to his eye
Whose look approving, oft as he returns,

For her illuminates and gladdens all.
Soon gorgeous Summer with light tread has passed;
And Autumn, laden with his fruits and sheaves,
Enrobed and garlanded with dying leaves
That dolphin-like grow beautiful in death,
Has hasted by, and seems a vision gone;
Winter with hoary head and frosty breath
Hath let loose all his storms, and the free streams
And yielding earth hath fixed as adamant.
Fled swiftly all; yet, in their passing, rich
In pleasures innocent and duties done;
In memories that, as treasures of the soul,
Shall live unfading down to distant years,
When, in life's twilight dim, quiescent age
Backward shall turn to wander o'er the past.
Then trod again shall be those evening strolls
In the still gloaming, or when climbed the moon,
While nature's kindliest influence softly stole
O'er each fond heart; lived o'er again shall be
Those fireside hours when each by turns or read,
Or eager listened to the thrilling tale,

To some old poet's lay, or ballad wild,
Or History's roll of deeds and men renowned.

But, blessed Home, these are not all thy joys;
Yet undiscovered are thy purest springs,
The streams untasted yet of holiest bliss
From wedded love by God ordained to flow.
Though now, ye favored pair, your cup seem full,
A gladder hour is nigh; a brighter star
Than e'er before your watchful eyes did greet
Now rises, o'er your path to shed its ray.
Hark! a new sound arrests the quickened ear!
A voice! a cry! — the cry of infancy!
Through every room it thrills; the very walls
That echo it, with sympathy seem touched.
A babe is born! Mother — O hallowed name!
Mary, that name is thine! close to thy heart,
Quick beating with a rapture all unknown
Till this blest moment, thou dost fold and press
Thy first born son! Thine anguish all forgot,
A joy so deep, so pure, so brimming o'er,

Possesses thy whole being, that to thee
It seems a new existence; ay, so strange
Thou almost deem'st it but a blissful dream
From which thou may'st awake. No — no!
Thou art a mother to eternal years!
Life of thy life, that helpless one is born
Immortal as the angels; by thy side
It shall still live when, as old seers have sung,
The ancient heavens have been together rolled,
And earth hath perished by devouring fire.
'Tis thine, for immortality, to guard and keep
The priceless treasure. Unto thee 'tis given —
No work of earth more sacred, more sublime —
That trembling spirit to insphere in love;
To fashion it by love's sweet ministries,
Till faculties yet hidden, full revealed,
Declare it fellow of the hosts of heaven!
No marvel if thy heart, at thoughts like these,
Doth falter, burdened with the mighty trust.

But not alone thou bear'st it. There is yet
Another holy name. Thou, Edward, art
A Father! — name like God's! a changeless name.
Thy manly soul, warmed with paternal love,
Calm, deep, and steady as a river's tide,
By this new life shall feel its own enlarged,
More joyous made and richer. Thou shalt find
In this, thy son, what seems another self;
Another centre, round which may revolve
Thy best affections and thy busy thought.
E'en while his infant prattle wakes the smile
Of fatherly delight, within thy breast
Grave questionings shall rise, with hopes and fears.
"How with thee shall it fare, unconscious child —
How wilt thou bear thyself, upon life's field
Where foe meets foe and wile encounters wile;
Where hapless thousands fall, or, wounded sore,
Survive but wrecks, unfit for noble tasks?
What destinies are thine? Wait there for thee
The shouts of triumph? or the pang and shame
Of final, sad defeat?" So wilt thou ask;

And then, with impulse new, thy soul will rise
To the firm purpose that in thee thy child
Shall find a model true, a wisdom pure;
Shall see a life well lived, and with thee walk
As one that breathes in virtue's bracing air;
As one divinely led, a child of heaven!

Father and Mother! holiest names of earth!
Lo! now, blest Home, thy circle made complete!
Thy pleasures full! Now, in each throbbing breast,
All sweetest chords, unstruck before, are touched;
Vibrations exquisite, that slept, awake,
And the whole compass of the soul pours forth
Harmonious pæans; as some organ full —
Drawn every stop — its perfect volume swells,
And with its faultless chorus charms the ear.
Yet o'er the world, to each fond parent's eye,
A nameless change has passed. A graver hue
Now tinges earth and sky, that laughed before
In flashing light and beauty ever gay.
Not less the light and beauty, nor the bliss

Of those beholding; but all things seem charged
With meanings deeper far, that needs must lend
An aspect chastened and a tone subdued
To nature's face, softer yet richer too.
Emotions now first waked, and loftier aims
Than e'er before had stirred the conscious soul
Write on each brow new dignity of thought.

As when is read some drama, rarely wrought
By genius' magic pen, the first act past,
That with strange power the attentive mind hath seized,
All note of time is lost, or heeded not,
While act on act succeeds till comes the last,
That disenchants the reader spell-bound long;
So when thy scenes, dear Home, divinely planned,
Have opened as if bathed in silver light,
Have cheerily swept on beyond the days
Of love's first raptures and the blissful hour
When felt the first-born's brow a mother's kiss,
The plot fast thickens, and intenser grow
The sympathies that fill and hold the heart,

Ever yet more content, while through quick years
The changeful action hasteth swiftly on.
One charming prattler scarce hath learned to lisp
The names most musical to infant tongues,
Ere yet another cherub face appears
In the pleased household, and in time's full round
Yet others still. Come added cares with each,
And duties new; but with such gushing love,
Such influx of deep joy, that all forgot
Or drowned in ecstasies, or tranquil bliss,
The weightier burdens seem. Life richer grows,
As, with the years, fair sons and daughters rise
In beauty fresh, like olive plants, to stand.

Father and mother! How their hearts expand,
As large, and larger yet, becomes the sphere
Where sweet affections reign; where brother blends
His rougher vigor with a sister's grace;
Somewhat each borrows and each somewhat lends,
And all, as one, true filial honor pay.
Home, thou art richer so than piled with gold

And rarest gems, yet wanting loving hearts;
Fairer than with all garniture bedecked
Of princely halls, with splendors cold, and pride.
If matched with thine, all other jewels pale;
E'en God himself with pleasure thine beholds.
Brothers and sisters! what blest concord binds
Congenial souls that breathe in virtue's air!
How are they knit by inborn instincts kind,
By common blood and birth, by childhood's sports
Together shared in many a shining hour,
By transient griefs, and alternations quick
Of hope and fear, that each has felt with all,
All felt with each. Concord more perfect made
By such slight discords as in all have wrought
More watchful tenderness of patient love.
More of thy strength, divine self-sacrifice!

Dwells then, O Earth, e'en in thy fairest spot,
A perfect bliss? Giv'st thou enduring joys,
Where nothing fixed abides? The circling years,
That swiftly chase each other in their flight,

Bring ceaseless change. Lo! Morning with her dews,
And songs and bloom; still Evening with her shades;
Sabbaths with holy calm, that yield too soon
To seasons given to rounds of wearying toil;
Months marked by waxing and by waning moons;
Spring with its waking life, Summer arrayed
In robes that fade so soon; Autumn that strips
The teeming fields, and leaves them brown and sere;
Winter that with his storms deep buries all
Kind Nature's smiles beneath his chilling snows!
Each comes but to depart, nor long abides.
See how like withering grass all beauty fades,
And strength to weakness turns; how the firm rock
Slowly, but surely, crumbleth back to dust;
How life's uncounted forms dissolve, O Death,
At thy cold touch that blighteth all alike!
Hath earth one spot so sheltered, so secure,
That there no change, no pang, no sense of loss,
No fear of ill, no sorrow, e'er can come?
No: even within thy precincts, sacred Home,
Must it at last be known that 'neath the sun
No mortal heart can beat and feel no wound.

Edward, what aileth thee, that anguish sits
Where smiles, like glancing lights, were wont to play?
Mary, thy cheek is blanched; thy restless eye
Turns frequent here and there, as if it sought
To rest on one with whom might come relief!
Ah, yes! a tender lamb of that fair flock
O'er which to watch hath been by day, by night,
Thy life's chief joy, now by the wayside droops;
Droops on from hour to hour; no skill avails
To cool the fevered brow, or light again
The languid eyes that kindle now no more.
In vain, O mother, have thy faithful arms
Enfolded him and pressed him to thy heart.
No care, nor yearning of maternal love,
Nor father's wrestling hope, can stay the step
Of Sorrow — awful form! — too clearly seen
Advancing; in her hands the cup of woe,
Of which 'tis given all mortal lips to taste.

'Tis o'er. Hark! Hark! soft on the startled ear
Music unearthly steals! celestial notes

And melodies, as from the airy lips
Of spirits all unseen, with mingled lyres
Touched as by angel fingers, seem to fill
The tranquil air. Ye cannot catch the strain,
But well ye deem that lovingly it greets
The gentle spirit of its clay disrobed.
Bear — bear the cherub, angels, to His arms
Who in his mortal years such lambs did fold
Close on his heart with heavenly grace and smiles,
And blessed and called them his, and said, — "Of such
Heaven's holy kingdom shall for ever be."
He hath its name already on his hands
Engraven, and hath watched it as his own;
And with a tenderness surpassing thine,
O mother, He thine innocent will meet,
Will soothe its fears and win its love with smiles
Of sweetness so divine that it shall need
No more e'en thy dear ministries, to fill
The measure of its bliss to full content.
What thou hadst thought to teach it, He will teach,
Of wisdom, goodness, beauty, truth, and love;

His care will guard and train it till the hour
When thou shalt come, the blessed day arrived,
With thine own eyes, long waiting, to behold
The vision of the Lamb. Back to thine arms
Then He the faithful Shepherd shall restore
Thy child — still thine — the same o'er which did fall
Thy bitter tears when lost to thee he seemed.
The same, yet not the same! more beautiful
Beyond compare, e'en as the hyacinth
That perfect stands, unfolded every grace,
Is lovelier than the bulb that held it once,
And hid its purple hues. Ah! then thy joy
The memory of thy grief at last shall drown;
And with all ecstasies of thankful love
And praise admiring, shall thy soul o'erflow.

He lies upon the bier, pale, silent, cold,
Yet beauteous still. Disease hath stolen away
But little from the face that late did seem
Almost a seraph's. On the marble brow
Chiselled so daintily, so calm, so pure,

Lies, as in carelessness, the flaxen hair.
In tranquil slumber one might deem he rests,
But that the leaden eye a sleep bespeaks
Too deep for waking. Folded on the breast,
Now motionless, repose the snowy hands
With flowers o'er-strown; strange contrast! e'en as when
Thick clustering violets are seen to spring,
Or lilies of the valley, where the drifts
Of winter part, touched by the vernal sun.
Mary, they saw thee come — and stand — and gaze —
As if thy soul, with anguish wrestling long,
At last had mastered its fierce inward strife;
As if a self-command that awful seemed
Had changed thee to a statue; saw thee take
Thy last, last look, and heard thy lips pronounce,
"My boy — thou'rt mine no more! I give thee back
To God who gave thee! O farewell! — farewell!"
So triumphed faith when anguish wrung the heart;
And as the rainbow spans the cloud o'erpast,
Emblem of peace that waits beyond the storm,

Thou saw'st with tranquil eye dark sorrow's gloom,
Irradiate with the glow of heaven's own light,
The pledge of days serene beyond these tears,
The harbinger of healing, rest, and peace.

PART III.

WOULDST thou from sorrow find a sweet relief?
Or is thy heart oppressed with woes untold?
Balm wouldst thou gather for corroding grief?
Pour blessings round thee like a shower of gold!
'Tis when the rose is wrapped in many a fold
Close to its heart, the worm is wasting there
Its life and beauty; not when all unrolled,
Leaf after leaf, its bosom rich and fair
Breathes freely its perfumes throughout the ambient air.

Carlos Wilcox.

THERE blend the ties that strengthen
  Our hearts in hours of grief,
The silver links that lengthen
  Joy's visits when most brief!
Then dost thou sigh for pleasure?
  Oh, do not widely roam!
But seek that hidden treasure
  At Home, dear Home!

Bernard Barton.

PART III.

O SACRED spot of earth, where gentle hands
Have laid the fragile form, so late suffused
With life's first glow, beneath the friendly mould;
To slumber undisturbed where daisies spring
Unbidden, and the turf, with every dawn,
Seems wet afresh with tears! There by fond hands
Ivy and myrtle have been taught to twine;
The snow-drop spotless and forget-me-not
To bloom in simple beauty, emblems meet
Of purity and of immortal love.
The friendly trees their drooping boughs o'erhang
As if in sympathy. The summer birds
Chant tender carols through the shining hours;
And mingled lights and shades so softly blend,
That neither garish day nor gloom doth reign,
But grateful twilight lingers ever there.

Dear, oft-frequented scene! 'Tis not that here
The sorrowing heart deems its lost treasure hid.
The living spirit that once blithely wore
The mortal robe that wasteth here to dust,
Dwells far, far hence, it knows, 'neath kinder skies.
But memories all undying centre where
This dust reposes, quick to stir anew;
Oft as with lingering steps this scene is trod,
The past is lived again; its bliss renewed;
And grief becomes but tenderness and hope,
Till o'er the heart there steals a holy calm,
And balm from heaven hath healed its bleeding wounds.

Toil is no curse to mortals; nor the cares
That make the price for life's best comforts paid.
Both have a charm — when on the saddened heart
Despondency and griefs, like clouds, have hung
Till into starless night day seems transformed —
The tide of ever busy thought to turn;
That winding ever farther, farther on,
Behind it leaves the dreariness and wastes;

And as, by slow degrees, new visions rise,
New scenes and aspects woo and win the soul;
Rekindle drooping hope and wake new joy;
Till — how one knows not — all along life's way
Sweet landscapes smile again and days are glad;
Welcome is duty's call, and future years
Invite to high endeavor, as they spread
Bright vistas opening far; and every pulse
With healthful beating tells the heart is strong.
Thou that hast suffered, brood not o'er thy woes.
But to thy tasks! Thy losses and thy pangs
Forget in cheerful toil; thyself forget.
There be who love thee yet; whom thou dost love;
For God and these still be it thine to live;
And, all unwearied, in love's ministries,
Go labor on and in thy works rejoice.

Edward and Mary! for you gather yet
Around the household board a ruddy band,
Like cluster roses that upon one stalk
Hang in their sweet luxuriance; some in bud,

Some just revealing a first crimson line;
Some half unfolded, some in their full bloom;
One charming whole, of diverse charms combined.
'Tis yours o'er infancy kind watch to keep;
To listen to the words half-formed that fall
From ruby lips just stammering to pronounce;
And childhood's shout and laugh, perchance its cries,
Since showers and sunshine fill its changeful day.
'Tis yours to note youth's impulses, that swell
With passion's rising flood the heaving breast
That resteth not, but yearns with vague desire;
That needs kind sympathy and wisest skill,
To cool the fever of fresh life that throbs
With pulses too intense, and shape aright
The forming purpose and aspiring aim.
To these high tasks returned, your faces wear
A smile of peace again, and hope's bright glow.
The missing, not forgot, hath been transformed
Into a precious jewel of the soul,
That, in the dear fidelity of love,
With many a pensive, many a pleasing thought.

Is kept with memory's holiest trusts enshrined.
Sometimes, perchance, when on the vacant chair,
Some childish plaything needed now no more,
Or garment laid aside, the eye may rest,
A sudden tear, a shaded brow, may tell
How in the constant heart still lives the lost.
Yet steadily again life's current glides
Along the wonted channels, where the banks
Wave, as of old, with woods and summer flowers,
And bees hum softly and the west wind plays,
And earth and skies once more are robed in light.

Childhood! thy bliss who hath not sung that e'er
The harp to tender melodies hath touched?
What is thy secret? What thy hidden joys,
So pure, so full, that left far, far behind,
In memory still they live; yea, dearer seem,
As hoary age through gliding years steals on?
E'en thy glad morning is not without clouds
That cast their gloomy shades. Not all unwet
With tears thy glowing cheeks; thy heart not free

From transient disappointments that corrode;
From chafing impulse and oft-crossed desire.
Yet art thou happy as the bounding fawn
That all day long, beside the lonely lake
And 'neath the arches of the forest deep,
Gambols at will, nor knows or want or fear.
Thy griefs abide not; soon the shadows flee
That cross thy path, and sunbeams gild again
Whate'er thine eye beholds, till all the world
For thee in gladness laughs, and sings for joy!
As yet thou canst not know the fretting cares,
The toils and weariness and bodeful fears,
The buffetings with dark misfortune's tide
O'erwhelming when too late for all retrieve.
These wait on ripened years. 'Tis meet that thou,
Dear child, to whom thy ignorance is bliss,
Shouldst drink the cup of innocent delight
Placed at thy lips, nor on the future draw
For aught to check thy heart's exulting play.

As in yon garden tastefully inhedged
And consecrate to beauty, rarest flowers
Of many a name thick clustering fill the place
That seems a realm, a kingdom, all their own,
Blending in rich variety their charms;
E'en so, O genial Home — secluded, made
By Heaven's kind law the nursery of joys
Only within thy loved enclosure known —
In thee all healthful pleasures, ever fresh,
Should spring abundant, and luxuriant grow
Filling all days and hours, and months and years,
With influences that wake and warm and cheer;
That send exhilaration through the soul,
And with refreshment bring a calm content.
Father and mother! yours the task to plan
With tireless constancy and thoughtful skill,
That boy, nor girl, for lack of joy at home,
Shall from the hearthstone turn and wander far
To quench at poisoned streams the thirst they feel.
Brothers and sisters — let each have their sports
By instinct chosen oft, if choice be given;

Sports such as best befit each sex and age
By nature's steady laws and inborn taste;
With others that together shared shall best
Give fresh young hearts delight, and make them bound
All joyously with sympathetic bliss.

Nor, O ye parents, let your hearts grow old;
As oft your breasts have throbbed with childish glee
And youthful ardors, yet remembered well;
Have felt the restlessness of keen desire
That seemed a quenchless thirst; still let them hold
Kind fellowship with new-born life and joy.
Be ye with childhood, children — youth, with youth;
Nor deem that aught of dignity, or grace,
Is lost by nursery raptures, heard afar
In echoing laughs and shouts from lisping tongues;
Scorn not to tell or hear the thrice-told tales
Of Fairies, Giants, and all monsters dire,
And chant quaint melodies, tradition's trust,
Safe handed down through generations dead!
Fail not when merry girlhood courts thy smile

With lips carnationed and her locks of gold,
To greet the baby house and black-eyed dolls,
Dressed and undressed and nursed through blissful
hours.
Frown not when roisterous boys or toss or strike
The bounding ball, or leap, or run, or ride
The mastered steed that, as the rider, loves
The rushing course; or when with ringing steel
The polished ice they sweep in winter's reign.
All pleasing pastimes, innocent delights,
That gladden hearts yet simple and sincere,
Let love parental gather round the Home,
And consecrate by sharing; let it watch
With kind, approving smiles each merry game
That quickens youthful blood, and, in the joy
That beams from crimson cheeks and sparkling eyes,
Its own renew, and live its childhood o'er.
So shall the scenes where life's fleet-footed years
Glide by with noiseless speed at last become
Memory's rich treasure-field, be all o'erspread
As with a radiant flood of golden sheen;

Such as, on cloudless days in eastern climes,
With the still, hazy air seems interfused,
Enrobing with a dreamy loveliness
All visible things, transfigured in its glow.
'Tis so that tottering age, with fading eye,
Still sees thee, childhood, glorious as of old,
And of all earth's delights thine last forgets.

But childhood's glory fades; its visions change;
For sweet simplicity and guileless trust,
Come youth's unrest, and thoughts that wider sweep,
With keener search and wishes reaching far;
And yearnings vague that crave they know not what;
Imaginations of all shapes and hues
That make earth seem a dreamland, and bright hopes
That in all gorgeous tints life's future limn.
Deep in the breast the sense of powers divine
Yet slumbering, stirs the eager soul with thirst
For wisdom's living streams, impels to curb
The impulses by pleasure's luring call
Awakened oft, and give to high pursuit

And silent solitude where knowledge dwells,
Long years whose disciplines may manhood yield.
Yes, Learning, 'tis of Home that thou art born!
Its needs demand thee and its tastes create.
Thy schools, thy classic halls and tranquil shades,
Haunted with memories of the nobly great,
Whose storied deeds and names that cannot die,
The pride of ages dead, enchantment lend
That seems like perfume breathed on all the air;
Where linger still the echoes ever sweet
Of lays renowned that Time's great bards have sung;
Where yet resound the words of fire pronounced
By orators who spake when balanced hung
On the swift moment destinies sublime;
Where, in fit gallery and alcove ranged,
Stand art's grand triumphs, wisdom's treasured lore,
All wonders most divine by genius wrought,
Of centuries the lesson and the light;—
These—these of household culture are the fruit;
Culture that early, as with heaven's own fire,
Inflames the generous heart; refines, exalts,

And with ambition's purest glow inspires
The youthful soul, not yet by sense enchained.*

O spectacle divine, where, heart to heart,
Father and mother, sons and daughters, blend
Their inborn sympathies in concert blest!
One body well compact by love's great law;
Each member fit, in its own native grace,
To fill the measure of the perfect whole.
Envies and jealousies, ye grow not here
Indigenous, as hated nettles spring
'Mid rows of marjory and beds of thyme;
Or if ye start — since e'en earth's fairest spot
Yields still some noxious weeds — are quick subdued,
As all unmeet to root and flourish thus.
Oft by attrition in its torrent bed
The precious gem may wear its roughness down,
Till from its polished surface back the beam
That brightly falls is thrown as bright again;
So generous souls in daily contact lose

---

* Appendix. Note C.

The excrescences of nature and the faults
That, left unheeded, must ere long become
Deformities, of God and man abhorred.

As year on year fulfils its circling round,
Thou, Edward, notest with a father's pride
Thy Edith's maiden charms that ripen fast
Toward fairest womanhood. Oft o'er thy heart
Steals there a tranquil joy, a deep delight,
As 'neath thy watchful eye that wearieth not,
New dignity and grace her form invest;
New beauty tints her cheek, new thoughtfulness
Sits on her brow and lends her beaming eye
A deeper meaning and a milder fire.
Thou, Mary, on thy Alfred lov'st to fix
With tenderness profound thy earnest gaze.
God-given was he in place of thy first-born,
That Christ desired and angels bore away!
So doubly dear; and now that in his face
Thou readest thoughtfulness, and seest revealed
Reason's calm light, and wakened intellect,

Imagination, hope, and purpose high;
Now that with quickened heart-throbs thou dost mark
His manly form and mien; whene'er thou wilt.
Dost find in him companionship, his arm
Thy strong support; his words a daily joy;
Thy mother's heart exults, nor would exchange
Its deep, deep bliss for Ophir's glittering heaps,
Or widest fame 'mid noisy contests won.
Thy woman's nature rests with full content
In these thy household treasures — asks no more.

How beautiful art thou, O Youth! Not lost
As yet in thee the sweetness and the grace
Of childhood left behind; but, richer far,
Thou wearest graces that are all thine own.
More full the sympathies that warm thy breast;
Thy thought more searching; keener far thy ken —
The vision of the soul athirst to know
Where hides true wisdom; larger thy desires
Far wandering, like the wanton summer winds
That rove o'er regions wide and dalliance hold

With all sweet odors, ever restless still;
Loftier thy purpose, more sublime thy thought
Than childhood ever knew, or e'er could know.
A youthful band — their souls all closely knit
In the pure love that of one blood and birth
By nature's law doth ever richly spring,
As from full fountains, in the cloistered Home,
A scene present on which e'en Heaven must smile.

Nor moves the round of household pleasures on
In dull monotony that needs must cloy.
Home hath its festal days — its holy times —
When fresh delights exhilarate; when Mirth
Seizes the sceptre and asserts her reign,
And Laughter, her prime minister, she bids
Wake rapturous echoes all her realm around!
When on affection's altar, with one will,
The gathered household their fresh offerings lay;
Intent that there, like holy altar fire,
Love's quenchless flame may ever brightly burn.

Dear old Thanksgiving! How the hallowed word
Restores, as in a moment, vanished years!
How back to life the honored dead it calls,
Whose hoary heads and venerable forms
The bounteous board of old were wont to grace!
They seem to come and sit and smile again,
And with their children's children share the joy.
How brothers, sisters, all companions dear
Of life's unclouded morn, together flow
From regions wide remote, and young again,
At least in heart, renew the scenes of yore!
This from the crowded city; that from where
The Prairie's naked bosom tempts the plough;
Perchance another, from beyond the flood
Where Mississippi pours his torrent down,
Or from fair Florida, beneath whose skies
Magnolias spotless open all their charms,
And orange blossoms scent the tranquil air.
But come they whenceso'er, they come to prove
Unlost, unweakened, the old love of Home.
Joy! Joy! Thanksgiving, that o'er all the land,
To-day a Nation's benison thou art.

And thou too, ancient festival, whose name
A word of joy through centuries hath lived —
Christmas! thou com'st with carols as of old
When angels chanted 'neath the midnight sky,
"Glory to God on high, good will to men!"
Methinks angelic choirs beyond the stars
Still warble round Messiah's throne the strain.
Earth well may lift her voice in jubilant praise
And all true hearts exulting greet the day
That tells the world anew the Christ is born!
Let holly, box, and fir tree lend their boughs,
Symbols of life immortal, to adorn
Each Christian temple. Ring, ring out, ye bells,
Sweet chimes that shall afar glad echoes start!
Then while the very air with love and peace
Seems all surcharged, within thee, happy Home,
Childhood and youth and hoary age may tell,
With many a gift and many a token kind,
With chastened merriment and generous cheer,
How beat in holy unison all hearts.
O Babe of Bethlehem! to Thee we owe

Home's dearest ministries and purest bliss.
Not less with mortal pleasures innocent,
Than mortal pains and tears, thy loving heart
Hath sympathy, for Thou art Goodness' self!

Next for the household comes the opening year
With greetings fervent, wishes true and kind,
From each to each, of countless happy days!
With the old year deep buried all neglects,
Now friendship's record, as on a fresh page
Unsullied, the New Year once more begins.
As with a chastened tenderness, farewell
Is said to the departed months, whose round,
On Time's great calendar, has been fulfilled.
Age, ripe in piety, with faith confirmed,
All thankfully recalls the past, yet still
Looks onward to the Father's House on high,
Well pleased the golden gates more near to see.
Childhood and youth, exultant, note how fast
Years bear them forward to the longed-for scenes
So gorgeous to their thought, of life's broad stage,

On which parts all heroic, as they dream,
Wait for their entrance, pre-ordained for them!
Nowhere, as where abides domestic love,
So richly "Happy" dawneth the New Year.

But best and dearest to the household comes
The day of holy rest; God's sabbath day;
From the world's early morning consecrate
To piety and peace, to prayer and praise,
And all the sanctities of worship paid;
To pleasures such as days of toil know not;
To love, the grace that the whole law fulfils —
Mother of virtues — of all thoughts and deeds
That to the pure in heart divinest seem,
And e'en to earth some semblance lend to heaven.
With the fresh morn, while grateful stillness reigns —
Stopped the great treadmill of the world awhile —
Parents and children meet with greetings kind
Around the wonted altar. The calm hour
No haste demands; and first to heaven ascends
In one sweet harmony, from joyful lips,

The Hymn that to the ear of Love divine
Tells of each heart's deep, fervent thankfulness,
More welcome than frankincense. Then the sire,
Priest of the family by God ordained,
From prophet old, or Psalmist, words of life
Reads reverently, as if afresh they came
From God's own lips to gladden trusting hearts;
Or lessons from His mouth who, Light of men,
Spake as no mortal tongue e'er spake besides;
Or from the story of his mighty deeds,
His lowliness, and grace that reached to all,
His shameful cross and wondrous sacrifice!
Then at the mercy-seat together bowed,
One tender voice, the worship of all hearts
Pours forth in utterance simple and sincere;
Forgiveness asks for common faults confessed,
And praise heartfelt, for blessings shared, presents
To Him without whom not a sparrow falls;
Life, health and comfort, all most dear, commit,
For coming days, to his o'er-watching care;
And 'neath the shadow of his wings to dwell

Entreats, one brief request including all.
So pass the peaceful hours. From morn till eve
Pleasures succeeding pleasures fill the day.
When the glad bells up to God's temple call,
With one consent the household join the throng
That tread the hallowed aisles, their hearts the while
Drawn to each other closer, while they rise
Godward in prayer and song, and hear the word
That life eternal tells. Then home returned,
With books and cheerful talk and songs that stir
All pure affections, the loved day they close.
Of sabbaths such as this the memories kept
Among the heart's best riches, shall remain
Till earth's last week shall end and brightly dawns
The endless sabbath, the sweet rest of heaven.

A time for all things — thus the wise man spake,
And — beautiful in its own time is each.
Not always, Edward, round thy bounteous board
Will greet thee youthful faces wreathed in smiles;
Not always, Mary, will thy quick ear hear

Mother ! — earth's dearest word — from morn till eve
Fall lovingly from many a coral lip.
Ye have been sowing long. With line on line,
Lessons of wisdom and of heavenly truth,
No season lost, it hath been yours to pour
Into fresh opening souls, that to receive
What from your lips distilled were ever fain.
Have ye not sought to form for virtue's tasks,
To shape to some true life-work, these the sons
And daughters given from God, your highest trust?
Draws nigh the reaping time. What most your hearts
For many a year have wished, your eyes shall see —
Your children, girded for life's contests high,
By Providence led forth. For this ye prayed.
Arrows not always in the quiver rest;
Fledged birds, not in the nest for ever stay;
Arrow, or bird, each at its hour must fly.
Onward — still onward — is the call divine
That all of mortal birth must hear and heed.
'Tis so that pleasures ever new are born
Out of new issues and oft-shifting scenes;

E'en things that most delight, unchanged should sate
From sheer monotony. Thy pleasures, Home,
Can only live through never-ceasing flow;
As brooks that hasten leaping, babbling on,
Are pure as crystal ever; but pent up,
Forbid their course to run, do stagnate soon,
And with green ooze breed noisomeness and death.
Ay, parents, send them forth, as God shall call —
Your best and dearest — not with fainting heart
And tears regretful, at what Home must lose;
But thankfully, since unto you 'tis given
To God and man offerings so rich to bring.

The gentle Edith ripe in maiden charms
Yet more and more the magic power reveals
Of cultured womanhood. Not wholly lost
The witching artlessness of childish years,
The airy freedom, the instinctive grace,
So winsome, till by fashion's hateful code
To chilling stiffness changed. Radiant she moves
Amid Home's cheerful band, in beauty's light,

As floats a planet in the evening sky,
Bright and still brightening as it higher climbs.
No bird of Paradise of plumage gay,
In thought or wish she seems; no trifler weak,
With vain conceit inflate, self-conscious, quick
With fluttering pulse to note each watchful glance
Of kindling admiration. Such as these,
Ye who would find may seek in fashion's halls,
Where dwell not Home's simplicity and truth.
Yet on her brow she wears, all clearly writ,
Intelligence; and in her beaming eyes,
The joyousness that tells a guileless breast
And yet unsounded depths of hidden love.
Parental hearts grow warm at sight of her,
And brothers look and worship. Oh, there's naught
Can touch so tenderly the restive soul,
Of youthful impulses o'erflowing full,
And urged by uncurbed will and passion's power
The tempter's voice to heed and choose the wrong,
As a fond sister's love, that wooes and wins,
Attempers what is wayward unto good,

And by its own pure effluence maketh pure.
Thou, Edith, art e'en as the warm south wind,
That, from the lips of Spring breathed o'er the fields,
Whate'er is loveliest waketh into life
With silent Power, till all are robed in bloom.
While Home thou blessest, thou thyself art blest.

Goodness, to beauty joined, is like the flame
That from the light-house on some towering cliff
O'er the wild waters throws its beams afar
At nightfall, welcome to the wanderer's eye.
Its glory streams abroad, nor can be hid;
But many an eye beholds it and admires.
Ah! maiden, thou that in thy freshness wear'st
With modesty and gentleness and grace
The charms that nature gave and goodness lends.
With power these charms invest thee — power perchance
Beyond thy utmost thought — to scatter wide
Influence that light and guidance both shall be
To many a heart sincere, that so inspired

Shall be by thee to nobler virtue won.
The power to bless by charming — wondrous gift!
How rich who hath it! How made like to God!
Woman, this most exalts thee and adorns;
Gives thee a sovereign sway, if so thou wilt,
And makes thee as a spirit of the skies.

To all, such Edith seemed. But most to one,
Young Arthur, from her childhood playmate, friend,
Sharer of frolic hours, and o'er the fields
And thro' the shadowy woods, when summer glowed,
Leader of many a ramble. Always kind,
Homeward from school her satchel oft he bore,
And through the winter snow her pathway trod;
Or cross the swollen brook, with friendly hand,
By the rude stepping-stones, he safely led.
With changing years advanced to manhood now,
Transformed he seems, yet not another made.
In manners courteous, almost distant grown,
Yet is he near her oft, with calm content
On his fair face clear written, and an eye

That back reflects her glance, as she for him
And he for her some secret fain would guard;
As if by some keen instinct each did read
The other's thought, to words not trusted yet —
Not uttered in full phrase — yet half expressed
Perchance not seldom, by some act or look,
Some pressure of the hand, some opening bud
Given to adorn the hair and meekly worn;
Some book together read, or some soft strain
In the still twilight by two voices sung!

There is a time to love! — a holy time
When from deep well-springs in the throbbing breast
Gush forth affection's purest, richest streams,
And flow unchecked, bearing through all the soul
Mysterious happiness; when fleet-winged thought,
As finished occupation sets it free,
To the loved being flies and lingers long —
As the wild bee, tasted the nectared cup,
Delays, and yet delays, its homeward flight —
Or, all impatient, in the busy hour,

Full oft it plays the truant and escapes;
Forgets all time and distance and afar
Seeks the secluded walk, or well-known bower.
O blissful season when the unfolding soul
Puts forth all sweet affections! when bright shapes
And visions, of imagination born,
And yearnings vague, and hopes, and wishes, blend
With a deep restlessness, that is not pain,
But rather seems a rapture; and all things,
The heavens, the earth, life's many shaded scene,
Past, present, future — future most — appear
Glorious, enchanting, in love's aureate light.
So in some grand cathedral, when the sun,
Through the stained windows, his full lustre flings
On priest and altar and the reverent throng
Of worshippers that crowd the solemn aisles,
'Tis as a new Shekinah filled the place,
And heaven's own splendors threw o'er all the scene.

She is betrothed! The changeless word is said!
Two souls are each to each for ever bound!

Is freedom then abjured — for bonds exchanged?
Arthur and Edith, each once free as air,
In thought, word, feeling, purpose, aim, and end —
Sold each a royal birthright when they sware
Henceforth to have one name, one life, one lot?
Or hideth seeming loss some priceless gain?
By somewhat yielded is it Heaven's great law
That the young heart, with conscious need disturbed,
Must find its fulness, what it restless craved?
Bound! Bound! Ah! thou that doubting askest — know
That unto thee love's mystery as yet
Is all unopened; thou art but a child!
Thou hast not learned how, in the blissful sphere
Where love triumphant reigns, a soul gains most
When most it loses; that when giving all
It takes all and is blest. Two hearts made one
In mystic unity of trustful love,
Constraint know not, nor liberty e'er lack;
With full consenting wills as one they choose;
Or differing aught, for this alone contend,

How each to other first and most may yield!
No bonds like thine do bind, O heaven-born love,
Yet as the angels free are loving souls!

Edith and Arthur, be the vernal days
Of your betrothal arched with azure skies
And glad with melodies of warbling birds!
Enchanting be the twilights, and the sheen
Of silvery moonlight on your evening paths!
Taste the dear joys of early love, and wait
In ecstasy delicious for the hour
When at the bridal altar blest ye stand.

PART IV.

Oh, hush the song, and let her tears
Flow to the dream of her early years!
Holy and pure are the drops that fall,
When the young bride goes from her father's hall;
She goes unto love yet untried and new —
She parts from love that hath still been true.

Mrs. Hemans.

How happy he who crowns, in shades like these,
A youth of labor with an age of ease!
Onward he moves to meet his latter end,
Angels around befriending virtue's friend;
Sinks to the grave with unperceived decay,
While resignation gently slopes the way;
And, all his prospects brightening to the last,
His heaven commences ere the world be past.

Goldsmith.

PART IV.

THE bridal came. The holy vows were said.
As on some April morn the changeful sky
Lets fall, e'en through the sunshine, fitful showers,
As each contending which the hour should rule;
So on that day alternate smiles and tears
On each face came and went. O Edward, thou
Thy struggling heart in vain dost strive to still;
Nor canst thou, Mary, when the sudden flood
Of gushing tenderness o'erflows thy breast,
Repress its heaving, or the quivering lip
At once compose, or dry the moistened cheek.
To-day a priceless jewel ye resign,
That has adorned your casket, flashed for you!
A heart that made sweet music in its beat
Of harmony with yours; an eye whose glance,
To you, like light from heaven, bore only joy!

Brothers and sisters, from your blissful bower
The full-blown rose ye loved is borne away,
Elsewhere to shed its fragrance. Yet grieve not,
As those who miss some treasure gone for aye.
Love chooseth ever what the loved shall bless,
And e'en in sacrifice finds sacred peace.
Edith but goeth, at the will of Heaven,
To kindle for herself a household flame
Whose light afar shall shine. Herself on all
Who in her bliss are blest, not less henceforth,
With Arthur at her side, shall gladness shed,
And to the Home she leaves shall not be lost.

As some prolific tree whose boughs with fruit
Bend earthward, yet through months of glowing suns
Keeps all its treasure till the harvest hour
Hath come at last; and, ripening once begun,
The process hastens till there naught remains
Save a bare gleaning on the plundered boughs
That look all lonely; so the Home where long
Young hearts have lingered, clinging each to each

And to the hearthstone where they first drew breath,
Must see them parted at the appointed bound.
When comes the day of ripeness and the spell
That held them one is broken, soon — ah! soon
The bands seem loosened all, and one by one,
Mature for life's high calling, goeth forth
With many a backward look and secret pang;
Till where but now there stirred a cheerful throng
Reigns the hushed quietness of emptied halls!
'Tis so, O Time, that thy resistless hand
With scene on scene the mortal drama fills.*

Alfred and brothers twain too soon are missed
When meet the household band. One burning heart
Hath kindled into generous passionate love
At Learning's shrine, by names illustrious fired
That, shining as bright orbs through ages gone,
Lit up the darkness, and for coming time
Together blended form a milky way
Glorious as that which spans night's ebon vault.

---

* Appendix, Note D.

In cloistered halls he hides for toilsome years,
Youth's passion curbs, its restlessness subdues,
And e'en as if to Learning's self betrothed,
Life's busy throng forsakes with her to dwell.
Another to the marts of hurrying trade
His steps hath turned; eager to tread where sweep,
Now this way and now that, the surging tide
Of rivalries that chafe and ventures high;
Where men for gain in life-long wrestlings strive,
Now win, now lose, and oft, ere manhood's prime,
Its sturdy strength wear out and die too soon.
Thrice happy they whose hearts die not, nor lose
All sweet humanities, though years be long
And crowned with rich successes all unstained!
Turns fondly to his mother earth a third,
By some deep impulse urged; and far away
Toward sunset regions he hath wandered forth
To fix his dwelling where beyond the flood
Broad Iowa her billowy bosom spreads.
There, 'neath his hand, the virgin soil shall soon
Grow genial, opened to the mellowing sun;

Quicken the scattered seed, and in its time
Reward the sower with the reaper's joy.
Around the new-made Home his tasteful hand
New beauties shall create. Well pleased his ear
Shall note the voices, echoing far, of flocks
And herds that 'mid abundance graze content;
Nor need he envy here the city's din
As glide, in healthful toil, the peaceful years.

Ah! Time, at once giver and robber thou!
Ere life hath reached its noon, each year beholds
Some gift possessed made richer, or some grace,
Some power, or pleasure, all anew bestowed.
But high noon passed, each year shall filch away
Somewhat of beauty's charm, of manhood's strength,
Of lustre from the eye, and from the ear
Of quickness to perceive the subtile thrill.
Thou stealest from the agile limb and step,
Elastic beyond art, the lithesome spring;
From golden locks, or raven, their bright hues
Thou plunderest silently, till all are gone;

And keen desire and love of high pursuit
And buoyancy of hope and courage firm
And aspiration restless evermore —
Whatever life's great tasks made seem but play —
So stealthily thou takest, that the robbed
Scarce note their loss, or noting half believe.
Yes, Edward, thou and Mary, yet thine own,
Still dear, far dearer, than when thy young heart
Felt love's first pulses beat, are not the same
In thought, wish, purpose, taste, or mien and air,
As when around you glowed the bridal morn.
The brows then fresh and fair, with deeper lines
Are furrowed by that skilled engraver Time;
Then life lay all before you, like some scene
Of rarest beauty to the eye made clear
And magnified by telescopic glass;
Now, through the glass inverted, ye behold
Reduced to littleness what once seemed great,
And dimmed, by half, the glory that did charm.
Grown calmer and more wise, ye, well content,
Resign your old ambitions, pleased to dwell

Amid Home's peacefulness, and with such tasks
As here the tranquil days may best beguile,
To wait till evening shadows gently fall.
Home hath not lost its sweetness — its content,
Though missed the cheerful voices, heard of old
Echoing through hall and chamber; though the night
Descend in solemn silence, where so oft
At close of day, for many a year, did float
On the still air enchanting harmonies.
No lonely hearts here dwell, that do but live
In sad, submissive patience, and earth's joys
For them all vanished deem, to come no more.

No — no! Not such the transformation wrought
By Time and Change, though wondrous be their power.
While creepeth stilly on life's closing scene,
And with the hoary head and trembling hand
Come signs of weariness, and for itself
Toil seems no more a pleasure; yet 'tis left
On the fled past to muse; and still to find
Companionship in books, or friends, around

The evening table where the loved were wont
Nightly to gather; or at will to sit
Beneath the old familiar trees that hang
O'erarching by the door, as long ago,
And seem of all things least to have changed with years.
Ay more — 'tis given to greet the oft return
Of children who, to filial duty true
And childhood's fresh remembrances, come back
To tread again the haunts for ever dear;
To hear grand-children's prattle and to watch
Their childish raptures as on grandsire's knee
They drink in, all attent, the well-told tale.
These are the tranquil pleasures left to age
When towards the sunset verges life's long day.
With these, deep in the trustful, loving soul
That 'mid life's turmoil walked by faith with God,
And, far above earth's ever shifting sands,
Builded on solid rock immortal hopes;
There come, as night draws nearer, glimpses oft,
And blest anticipations, of the realm

For ever fair, beyond the rolling spheres,
Where years no more shall ravish youth away,
Nor love be parted from its loved again.

Edward, thy Mary's voice for thee has lost
Naught of its sweetness; it delights thee still,
Like old familiar music. On that brow,
Mary, that in its manliness did charm
Thy girlhood's eye, not less thou lovest still
To gaze, though o'er it age hath spread his snows.
Ah! richer now, in either breast, the flow
Of love's pure current, than when ye did speak
With trembling ecstasy the marriage vow
Before God's altar. Then that current welled
From confidence and hope; from knowledge now,
And mutual virtues tested, till, like gold
Fresh from the crucible and proved by fires,
They shine with lustre that no doubt can dim;
Blest in each other, ye are doubly blest.

Nor are ye lonely left. One daughter still,
Fair Ella, youngest of the household band,
Like some bright minister of heavenly love,
Each morning greets you, fresh herself as morn,
And watches, all the day, if she may read,
In look, or motion, even your rising wish!
Or with some sweet surprise may light a smile
On your calm reverend brows, perchance provoke
To merry laughter, never hard the task.
A kind good-night she says when silent hours
Call you to tranquil sleep. Good-morrow sweet
She bids you with each dawn. For you she lives;
Herself forgets; forgets the brilliant halls
Where Fashion holds her court, ever best pleased
With acts of filial duty done, she seems.
Nor till her eyes shall see you pass the gates
Of life eternal, shall aught else divide
Her constant heart, whose every beating pulse
Tells that for you her very life-blood flows!
O faithful love! that, self-devoted, deems

All toil and care for you a mighty debt,
And to the utmost, the full score would pay!

Yes, woman! Though oft-times to thee 'tis given
Thy heart-kept hopes, at duty's call, to yield
All cheerfully; for God and those that else
Were left forlorn and loveless, thine to make
The lot of those who nobly much resign;
Though thy life's course be like a modest stream
That through the vale in grateful coolness winds,
And hidden half, with tree and bush o'erhung,
Freshness exhales e'en when itself unseen;
Though Providence, or thine own choice, deny
The household throne and dear connubial bliss,
Yet beautiful and blest thy life may be;
Rich in self-culture, and each grace and charm
Of mind, or manners, loveliest in all eyes;
And filled with deeds that the recording pen
Shall chronicle in heaven. The world yet teems
With griefs and groans; with pierced and bleeding
hearts,

To stanch whose wounds there needs the hand of love;
With sin, and souls debased, and dark despair;
With ignorance perverse and error blind;
With mercy's tasks untold, that well befit
Thy delicate fingers and thy facile skill;
On thee it calls, and wide before thee spreads
Such fields where love's best triumphs may be won,
As make it grand to live and toil and bear.
If thou wilt be a trifler, deep the shame!
If frivolous and vain, with all the gifts
Of God conferred to make thee seem divine,
Demons must clap their hands in fiendish glee,
And pitying Goodness turn in tears away!
Be a true woman, whatsoe'er thy place,
In solitude, or crowd, or youth, or age,
And life shall be to thee no joyless waste,
But rich in pleasures that sate not the soul.
Thyself revere; nor suffer without need
Thy robes to draggle in the common dust!
Be as God would — in thine own sphere a sun,
And round thee glorious planets shall revolve,

Glow in thy light, and life and comfort find.
So shalt thou bless thy kind, and all shall gaze
Admiring, and like Parsees worship thee!

As in late autumn, when the frosty earth
With withered leaves is strown, the forests bare,
And many a signal tells drear winter nigh,
Comes Indian Summer with her gentle reign
And charms which, tempered by the golden haze,
Half veil and half transfigure Nature's face
That with pale, pensive beauty still delights,
As peacefully go by the tranquil days;
So while age ripens, and when whitened locks
And the dimmed eye and faltering step forewarn
That not now distant lies the vale of shades
Earth's darkness parting from eternal day,
Full oft there comes a season all serene,
Whose sunshine mellowed falls, whose airs are mild
As softest breath of May, whose tempests sleep,
Whose peace is like the Sabbath stillness, when
A hushed world waits and worships. 'Tis as if

O'er the calm spirit silently there steals
Some effluence celestial, that inbreathed,
As from the throne of God, a baptism seems
Of love divine, before the mortal strife,
The waiting soul from ties of earth to free,
And heavenward lure her towards her coming bliss.

'Tis in this hallowed time that Edward now
And Mary, side by side, like ripened sheaves
With yellow grain rich laden, bide the hour
When the great Husbandman with faithful care
Shall bring them to his garner. Ella's hand,
With love's instinctive gentleness, delights
To bear for them each burden, and each day
Some pleasure new to bring. The furrowed brow,
Soothed by her touch, seems ever half to lose
Its look of weariness; and at her voice,
Whose tones are cheering as the morning lark's,
The languid eye grows brighter; and the ear
Tires not that listens to her pleasing talk,
Or readings, that beguile the loitering hours;

The genius of the place, she lives and moves
Like some kind ministering spirit of the skies,
Sent forth the aged pilgrims Home to lead.

But mortal years must end. Mary, thy cheek
So touched with crimson once, now paleness wears;
Falter thy footsteps on the lengthened path
Where thou of old didst tread like the gazelle
That scaleth with fleet limb the mountain side;
Faintness invades thy heart, so wont to beat
With ardor healthful and with purpose brave.
Beside thee bends thy Edward's reverend head;
Grieved not for thee, so soon to see His face
Whose beauty to behold ye both have pined;
But for himself, that he may not as yet
Enter within the veil, but without thee,
Still in the outer court must linger lone.
Thy children too, Edith and Arthur soon,
Then those who dwell afar, in hurried haste,
With Ella, gather in the chamber hushed,
And watch the failing pulses. O dread hour,

When hearts long loving and in love made one
Are each from other rudely rent away!
Yet Faith can triumph here, and calmly say —
"Thy will be done!" can hear the symphonies
Soft floating on the air, from unseen harps,
That welcome to the invisible host of God
Another sister spirit, pure and free!
She is translated — and with Christ abides!

Edward, not long shall Earth detain thee now!
Her lights grow dim, and like a vision fade
Her transient glories; heavenward look thine eyes.
Thou wouldst not linger, and the hour is nigh
When thou shalt hear kind voices bid thee — come!
And see, beyond the flood, thy Mary stand
With arms outstretched to beckon thee away!
Then, Ella, thy dear, loving hand shall close
Thy father's dying eyes; that placid brow
With thy last filial tears thou shalt bedew,
Thy filial tasks all done. Then farewell Home!
Thy Home from infancy, through long, long years,

Whose histories upon thy soul are writ,
As if, with iron pen and diamond point,
Graved on the eternal rock. Go, thou true heart,
Well trained by duty for all holiest deeds!
Go forth where sin lays waste and sorrows spring,
And round thee scatter gladness, light, and joy!
In thee let it be seen that woman, true
To love's best impulses, must needs command
All honor from the world, by all revered.
So shall thy name enshrined in grateful hearts
Be as a jewel kept; and thou at length
Shalt hear the Ever-blessed say — Well done!
And pass the threshold of thy Father's House,
The Home of Homes where changeless love abides!

O haste the happy day when o'er the world —
The wide, wide world — bright altar fires shall burn
On household shrines all countless as the sands!
When homeless thousands shall no more be found
Far scattered without shepherd, wandering sheep
Unpitied, left of savage beasts the prey!

Ye who with ruthless hand would madly tear
From the chaste maiden's brow the marriage wreath,
The sanctities destroy that God ordained
To guard domestic joys; the springs would taint
Of pure affection and foul lust unchain
To work its will till Homes are known no more;
Could the base wish succeed, the race undone,
And conscious of its wrong, on you would pour
Its curses without measure — well deserved!
Religion's ministers! lift up the voice
On your high watch-towers, and assert His law
Who to unbind what God hath joined forbade.
Statesmen! loose not with sacrilegious hand
The holy tie without which perish Homes.
Know that when Homes shall perish states shall fall,
And earth, e'en as the nether world, be hell!
The citadel of hope for earth is Home:
Home the best type that earth affords of Heaven.

Yes! though like all beneath these changing skies,
The joys of Home abide not; though itself

By its own law dissolve, when circling years
Have finished, one by one, its shifting scenes,
And sundered far the hearts once closely knit;
All ends not here. Hath not the Master said
That in his Father's House, for loving souls
Are many mansions, whither safely led,
And made one family, they shall with Him
Their Elder Brother dwell, for ever one?
There the great anti-typal palace waits,
Thronged with the sons and daughters of our God
Made like unto the angels; and the feet
Of all the pure in heart shall thither come.

O mortal! whatsoe'er thy lot hath been,
If, half bewildered, thou hast seemed to stray
A homeless wanderer o'er a barren waste,
If one that much hath loved and much hath lost,
Or one that loveth much, and much doth fear
What most he loves to lose; let thy stilled soul
Repose itself in peace. Though on thy head
Fierce tempests frequent beat, and all too oft

Clouds, dark o'ershadowing, veil the cheerful skies,
And gloom brood o'er thy path; though round thy
steps
Perils thick-clustering wait; though cares oppress,
And each day hath its strifes, and Sorrow pours
From her exhaustless flagon for thy lips
Full cups of bitterness; though life's best joys
Seem half to lose their sweetness, and no more
Enkindle keen desire, nor yield delight
To the tired sense, worn with the round of years;
Still be thou calm! Be strong and falter not!
Teach thy chafed spirit, that, in weariness,
Pants for her rest and longs for wings to soar
To kinder skies beyond this land of storms,
Her restless thoughts to stay; and in the strength
Of Hope, that, like the needle, trembling oft,
Is steadfast still, to wait the coming hour
When she well pleased the mystery shall read
Of earth's stern disciplines. Then on thine eyes,
Beaming with life immortal, full shall break
The wonders hidden long. Then Love Divine

Wide open the effulgent gates shall fling,
And bid thee enter; there, beside the throne
Where sits the Lamb, shall show thee the bright Home,
For Him and his for ever dear redeemed
Builded of God ere yet the worlds were made.
Lift, lift thy glance, O mortal, troubled, sad,
And lose thy griefs and fears in thoughts of Heaven!

There wait thee solid joys. What most thy heart
Hath yearned to find, yet ever sought in vain
Through perished hopes and crosses ever new —
Sweet rest, with full content — thou there shalt know.
Thy cup of blessing filled, thou shalt behold
Divinest splendors, all things bright and fair;
With which compared, earth's purest loveliness
Remembered shall all unsubstantial seem,
A shadow and a type. Thy treasures lost,
By stern Death wrested from thy warm embrace,
Now clothed in spiritual beauty and complete
In all celestial graces, still thine own,
There thou again shalt find. Theirs the old love,

Changed only as made richer in its flow
And deeper far; as if, checked for a time
By separation, it the while had swelled,
Till ready, like a flood, to force its way.
These shall such greeting give thee as shall thrill
Thy raptured spirit, ne'er again to know
Unquenched affection's thirst; while high above
Thou seest writ in words of flashing light:
"No pang, no death, no partings, evermore!"

Heaven! 'Tis no misty dream. What mortal eye —
Unlifted yet the veil — hath never seen,
Nor can, with keenest glance; what mortal ear,
Though listening all attent, hath never heard,
Even in faint echoes, God himself hath shown
To loving hearts and true. By visions clear
And words celestial, whispered soft and sweet
In the rapt spirit's depths, revealed have been
Mysteries of life and beauty, love and joy,
That from of old await the sons of God,
Their heritage, reserved till their glad feet

Shall pass thy gates, Jerusalem the New!
In Thee, O Holy City, crowned with grace,
Builded of gems imperishable, with walls
Of adamant that sin and woe debar,
O'erarched by skies serene without a sun,
And watered with pure, living streams, that flow
For ever from beneath the Mount of God —
In Thee, fulfilled, and more, each promise stands.

Nor this alone. For lo! the Lamb himself
From the eternal throne — where "in the midst
As one that hath been slain" He yet appears,
Wielding all princely power o'er earth and Heaven,
With "many crowns" on that once bleeding Head —
Full oft descends, with gentlest mien, to walk
All lovingly, a Bridegroom with his Bride,
Rejoicing o'er her in her bridal robes,
White as the light and lustrous as the sun.*
In dear companionship amid the throng
By his own pangs redeemed, now tenderly

---

* Appendix, note E.

He talks of Golgotha, the tomb, the morn
When the rent sepulchre resigned its trust,
And He triumphant, first-born from the dead,
Death's sceptre broken, trod the earth again;
When his own saw Him, heard Him, and believed
That He, whom on the tree they saw expire
In agony and shame, was LORD OF ALL!

Ah! how their blessed spirits now respond
In rapturous praise, and thanks, and burning love —
Love that not blindly burns, like theirs of old
Who to Emmaus walked — while heavenly words
Fall like soft music from those lips divine!
His glory they behold, that glory share,
Even as on earth he said. All human grace
With the full Godhead's dignity combined,
And lowly gentleness, enrobed He seems
With beauty infinite! They, all intent,
And ravished, gazing on his unveiled face —
O vision long desired — themselves transformed
And in his likeness made, exultant see;

To know as they are known supremely blest.
He feeds them — He whom seraphim adore!
He leads them where eternal fountains rise,
That they may thirst no more; and from the eyes
That wept on earth so oft, his loving hand
All tears hath wiped for evermore away.

APPENDIX.

APPENDIX.

NOTE A.

NOTHING could well be more uncandid than the representations of a certain class of writers in their attempts to disparage the Fathers of New England. It is not wonderful that some errors of past ages and of their own age were still revealed in them. It is not strange that having left their native land and endured all sacrifices for the sake of enjoying their own opinions unmolested, they should have been sensitive to the intrusion of new elements of strife. That they misjudged and acted wrongly in some particulars is readily to be admitted. But that even their faults "leaned to virtue's side" only ill-nature and prejudice can deny.

"It was in self-defence," says the historian Bancroft, (History United States, p. 463) "that Puritanism in America began those transient persecutions of which the excesses shall find in me no apologist; and which yet were no more than a train of mists hovering, of an autumn morning, over a fine river, that diffused freshness and vitality wherever it wound. The people did not attempt to convert others, but to protect themselves. *They never punished opinion as such;* they never attempted to punish or terrify men into orthodoxy. The history of religious persecution in New England is simply this: The Puritans established a government in America such as natural justice warranted, and such as the statutes and common law of England did not warrant; and that was done by men who still acknowledged the duty of a limited allegiance to the parent state. The Episcopalians had declared themselves the enemies of the party, and waged against it a war of extermination. Puritanism excluded them from its asylum. Roger Williams, the apostle of "soul liberty," weakened the cause of civil independence by impairing its unity; and he was expelled, even though Massachusetts always bore good testimony to his spotless virtues. Wheelwright and his friends, in their zeal for strict Calvinism, forgot their duty as citizens, and they also were exiled. The Anabaptist, who could not be relied upon as an ally, was guarded as a foe. The Quakers denounced the worship of New England as an abomination and its government as treason, and therefore they were excluded on pain of death."

Elsewhere (Vol. I. p. 454) Mr. Bancroft writes, — "Some of the Quakers were extravagant and foolish. They cried out from the windows at the magistrates and ministers that passed by, and mocked the civil and religious institutions of the country. *They riotously interrupted public worship;* and women, forgetting the decorum of their sex and claiming a divine origin for their absurd caprices, smeared their faces *and even went naked through the streets.*" It was for these gross violations of public order and decency and the rights of other people, and not for their religious opinions, that they suffered.

The historian further says: "The effects of Puritanism display its true character still more distinctly. . . . Puritanism was a life-giving spirit; activity, thrift, intelligence followed in its train; and as for courage, a coward and a Puritan never went together.'

Again, the same pen writes, — "Of all contemporary sects the

Puritans were the most free from credulity. . . . So many superstitions had been bundled up with every venerable institution of Europe, that ages have not dislodged them all. The Puritans at once emancipated themselves from a crowd of observances. Hardly a nation of Europe has as yet made its criminal law so humane as that of early New England. A crowd of offences was at one sweep brushed from the catalogue of capital crimes." So other standard historians.

It is a sin alike against the memory of the greatly good and against truth and Christian charity, to attempt to hide beneath a few mistakes the most exalted virtues.

NOTE B.

The Anglo-Saxon race have everywhere exhibited strong social affections, and among them have been found, to a greater extent than among those of any other race, examples of well-ordered, intelligent, and virtuous homes. But even in England the number of such homes in proportion to the entire population is small. They are not relatively numerous beyond the circle of the aristocracy of rank and wealth. But among the Anglo-Saxon population of our older States the proportion of such homes is large. You can hardly go into any respectable looking farm-house in Massachusetts or Connecticut without finding on the parlor table, along with the Bible, the works of Shakespeare, Milton, Addison, Johnson, Cowper, Wordsworth, and other eminent writers, and seeing many other indications of a degree of intellectual and social culture not extensively found among the common people of any other land.

NOTE C.

The writer believes most fully that he has not overstated this matter in the text. The desire for the intellectual development of their children, so that they may become qualified to bear some honorable part in the great activities of life, is one of the strongest of parental instincts. Our fathers shewed how powerful it was in them by founding schools and colleges almost before they had secured for themselves the ordinary comforts of life; and with patient care they began the course of education in the family. Yale, Harvard, and other institutions, not only originated in parental solicitude, and tastes and impulses nourished in the household, but are largely dependent on these to-day, and always must be.

NOTE D.

The dissolution of the family by the going forth of its younger members one by one to the tasks of life, though it is always a sad process in itself, has yet its compensations. The happiness, the enduring welfare of the child, becomes to the thoughtful parent the paramount consideration. When, therefore, children go forth from beneath the paternal roof under favorable auspices, the pang of surrendering them is materially mitigated; and if they are seen living usefully and well, and especially if they rise to eminence among the wise and good, parents cannot but find in this a rich and abiding satisfaction that in large measure compensates for the loss of their society.

NOTE E.

The poet Burns, though he went to an early grave the victim of his own appetites, exhibited often an exquisite appreciation of what was morally beautiful and touching. In one of his letters he writes that he could never read without tears the following text from the New Testament:—

"The Lamb which is in the midst of the throne shall feed them, and shall lead them unto living fountains of waters; and God shall wipe away all tears from their eyes."

Cambridge: Press of John Wilson and Son.

CPSIA information can be obtained
at www.ICGtesting.com
Printed in the USA
LVHW030145210323
742063LV00002B/768

9 783382 129583